Copyright © 2021 by Ollie Parker Publishing, LLC

"Everybody Porks: A Humorous Guide to the Birds and Bees for Parents and Their Inquisitive Children". All rights reserved. No part of this book may be used or reproduced in any manner whatsoever without the express written permission of the author, except in the case of brief quotations embedded in critical articles or reviews. For further information, please contact Ollie Parker Publishing, LLC at 30 N Gould Street, Ste R, Sheridan, Wyoming, 82801.

Illustrated by Rezdewi Studios

ISBN (paperback book) 978-0-578-88905-4
ISBN (e-book) 978-0-578-88889-7

To my wife Patricia, for all of your help and guidance throughout this process. This would not have been possible without you, moja droga kochanie.

To our friends and family for all of their belief and support. We sincerely thank you all!

To bourbon for giving me the liquid courage to put e-pen to e-paper. You are as wise as you are delicious.

Finally, to our daughter, Mila. You are the sunshine in our lives. That said, I hope you never ask me this question...ask your mommy sweetie, ask your mommy.

Momma, I have a question.

I was wondering...where do babies come from?

Well...

You may hear that babies grow in patches
Or that they're brought by storks
But the truth my little piglet dear
Is that everybody porks!

Wait, so parents "make" babies?
How does that work?

We shared a kind of special hug

Which sounds a little funny

But it let you grow up nice and snug

Inside your Momma's tummy!

Okay ... but, how did that work for you and Poppa?

Good question!
We had a romantic dinner
Surrounded by candle lights and wine
Then went dancing out on the town
And had a grand ole' time!

We came back home, all alone
Both our hearts were quaking
Your Poppa got to baby zone
Once momma shook her bacon!

I think I understand.
Now is it the same for everyone?
Do their parents "make" them too?
What about Charlie Beaverton?
What did his parents do?

I am glad you asked!

The Beavertons make dams
That stop water, like a cork
But to make their little Charlie
They would surely have to pork!

It's the same for lots of the animals, my dear

For example...

Kitty cats may pork

In the alley ways

While Porcupines will pork
Very carefully!

Bunny rabbits pork
And pork until they're sore

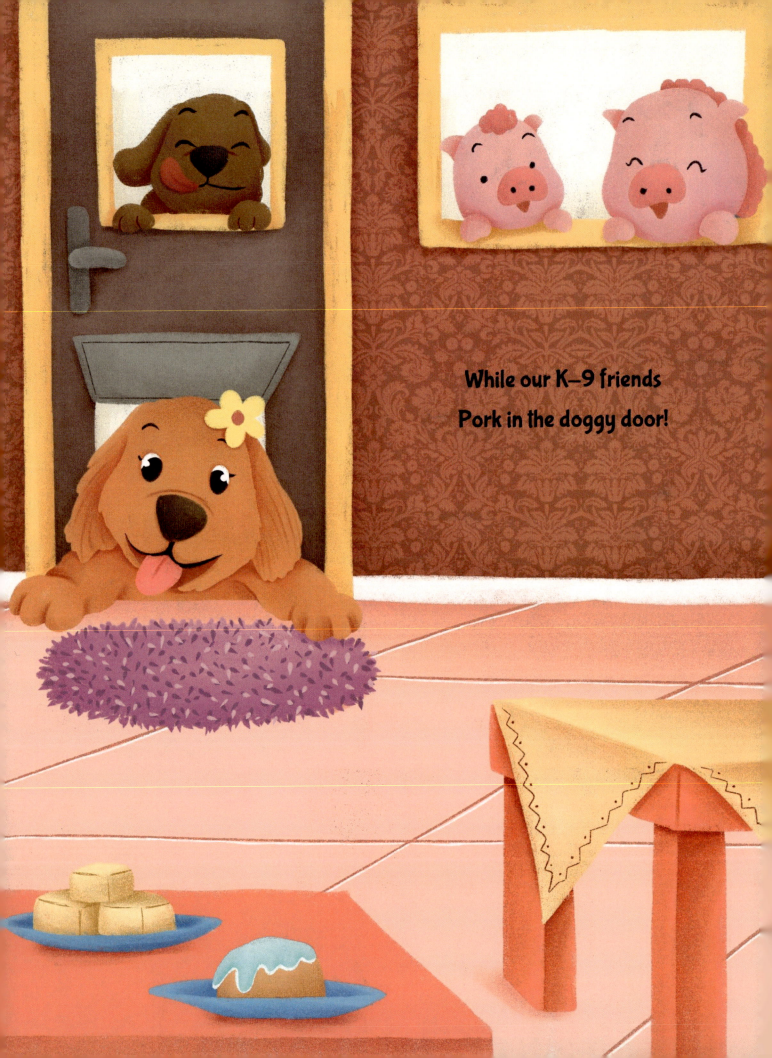

While our K–9 friends
Pork in the doggy door!

Hmm ... What about animals from really far away?
Do they "make" their babies the same porkin' way?

They sure do!
Let's take a look at some!

Cheetahs' pork with lightning speed
Regardless of the mama's needs!
Before they even blink an eye
A baby cub will soon arrive

I swear this never happens!

Giraffes may get a little freaky
They are tall but very sneaky
They like to hide where no one sees
With their heads above the trees

Papa monkeys pound their chests
To show the tribe that they are strong
They'll even flash their rumps to stress
That porkin' time has come along

And bears who carry tons of weight
Will pork until they hibernate!
Cuddled up all nice and snug
Making their own "bare-skin" rugs

Moving on to wood peckers
Who make loud noises with their beaks
Some may call them tree wreckers
But they're just making baby peeps!

peep, peep

Even skunks pork just the same
But heed my warning when I say
If they're close; we hold our noses
Because it will not smell like roses

What about the sea creatures?
They have to do it differently.

While they have different features.
They pork just like your Pop and me!

Think of giant sea turtles
Who do it in the seas and swells
They overcome some big hurtles
But really come out of their shells

Just a few more minutes, I'm almost there!

Dolphins like to swim and play
Their favorite game is 'Hide and Seek'
But when it's baby making day
You may hear them yell "Eek! Eek!"

Thanks Momma.

I cannot wait to ask others if they pork!

Not so fast!

Remember, we all may pork
At many times, in many places
But if you ask a stranger that
They will surely give you funny faces

All you need to know for now

Is the question "Where?" not "How?"

What matters more than all above

Is where babies come from...and that's from love

Those porcupines were funny.

Yes they were dear, yes they were.

Made in the USA
Middletown, DE
06 May 2021